Kalki Mahakal

Sri Joydip

Dedication

Mahakaleswara

Book Name: **Kalki Mahakal**

All global publishing rights are held by

Sri Joydip Ashram
93 Itbhata Road, Burdwan -713103
http://srijoydipashram.wordpress.com
editor.subhadip@gmail.con

Published on 25th Jan 2026

Kalki Mahakal

Sri Joydip

Statutory Warning / Legal Disclaimer

This book, “Kalki Magakal” is a work of fiction and creative imagination inspired by ancient narratives from the Mahabharata.

All characters, dialogues, locations, and sequences of events presented herein are products of the author’s imagination. Any resemblance—direct or indirect—to real persons, living or dead, or to actual institutions, organizations, or social groups is purely coincidental.

While certain ideas, symbols, and philosophical elements from the Mahabharata have been reinterpreted in the context of modern society and politics, this work represents a contemporary retelling from an entirely new perspective.

The purpose of this work is not to offend or hurt the sentiments of any religion, community, historical, or mythological figure, but rather to inspire reflection on the modern relevance of ancient wisdom.

Readers/viewers are requested to engage with “Kalki Mahakak” purely as a literary and artistically constructed work of fiction.

Kalki Mahakal

Sri Joydip

Contents

Introduction

Book Summary

Chapter One: The Black Mountain Calls

Chapter Two: The First Omen

Chapter Three: The Mantra He Never Learned

Chapter Four: The One Who Should Not Be Named

Chapter Five: The First Trial Is Silence

Chapter Six: The refusal to become Kalki

Chapter Seven : Meeting Sutapa

Chapter Eight: Kolkata - The City Where Silence Is Impossible

Chapter Nine: The Weapon That Refuses a Hand

Chapter Ten: The Woman Who Knows the Seals

Sri Joydip Ashram course path

Author Bio

Introduction

Kalki 2028 ends with the awakening of a question; Kalki Mahākāl begins with the arrival of an answer.

In an age when Kali's shadow has seeped into institutions, relationships, and even faith itself, Suranjana and Subimal become unlikely vessels of a cosmic turning point. From their union is born Kalki—not as a thunderous miracle witnessed by crowds, but as a silent child cradled in secrecy, vulnerability, and danger. His birth is marked not by celebration, but by omens: collapsing moral orders, trembling rivers, and a sky that refuses to remain indifferent.

Knowing that mere birth does not make an avatar, Kalki is taken to the timeless domain of Mahākāl—where time dissolves, ego is burned, and truth remains naked. There, the child-ascetic undergoes an intense tapasya that is as inward as it is terrifying. Mahākāl does not bless easily. Kalki is stripped of comfort, memory, and even identity. He confronts fear, doubt, compassion, rage, and the temptation to become what he must destroy. Only when he learns mastery over time, death, restraint, and righteous violence does Mahākāl grant him his divine boons—not weapons alone, but discernment, patience, and the burden of irreversible choice.

Kalki Mahākāl is not merely the story of a coming war; it is the chronicle of preparation. Kali is not defeated by force alone—he thrives on chaos, manipulation, and moral confusion. Kalki must therefore become more than a warrior; he must become a mirror in which humanity sees its own decay.

As the world moves unknowingly toward its final confrontation, Kalki steps out of Mahākāl's realm—no longer a child, not yet a savior, but a conscious force aligned with cosmic law. The war with Kali is inevitable. But before blood is shed, time itself must be corrected.

The countdown to the last battle begins.

Book Summary

Kalki Mahākāl begins in silence rather than spectacle.

Suranjana and Subimal give birth to Gopal away from the public gaze, in a world already dominated by Kali's invisible reign. The child is not celebrated; he is hidden. For in this age, truth must first survive before it can be proclaimed.

Unlike traditional avatar narratives, Gopal he is considered child Kalki does not immediately assume divine authority. He must earn it. Taken to the timeless realm of Mahākāl, the lord of time and dissolution, Kalki undergoes an intense tapasya that strips him of identity, attachment, and even certainty. Mahākāl tests not his strength, but his restraint; not his power, but his capacity to bear responsibility without ego.

Through metaphysical trials and existential confrontations, Kalki receives his divine boons—clarity of time, mastery over death, and the discernment to distinguish righteous violence from vengeance. These are not gifts of triumph, but burdens of irreversible consequence.

As Kali consolidates power across institutions and minds, the novel moves toward an inevitable war—not merely physical, but ethical, psychological, and civilizational. The final act where Gopal travels to Kolkata from where Kali he prepares the stage for a conflict that will decide whether humanity evolves or collapses into repetition.

Kalki Mahākāl is the story of becoming—not a god descending, but a consciousness rising to meet destiny

KALKI MAHĀKĀLA

Chapter One: The Black Mountain Calls

The white garment shimmered in the half-light.

Wrapped in a plain white stole, with a thin line of intricate embroidery at its edge, the figure seemed to glow from within. The light did not merely fall upon him—it emerged from him. His face carried the clarity of youth, yet behind it rested something older, deeper, almost timeless.

All around him rose black mountains, silent and unmoving. Among them, he stood like a single flame in a field of shadows.

This was the path Gopal walked every day.

But “home” was not merely a house. It was Jñānagañja—a forgotten land of wisdom where sages, ascetics, and siddhas once came to meditate. Even now, the air held an unnatural stillness. Sound itself seemed reluctant to enter.

At the heart of a narrow valley stood two mountains.

One was white.

One was black.

As a child, Gopal had heard the story from Chitrarath-da.

“The black mountain,” he had said, “is Mahākāla himself.

The white one beside it is the Śivaliṅga Mountain.”

From that moment, something inside Gopal had shifted.

The black mountain did not merely stand there.

It called.

Not with sound—but with presence.

People whispered that powerful ascetics lived near it. Worshippers of primordial energy. Men who had crossed thresholds ordinary humans never dared to approach. Once, his mother had forbidden him to go near the mountain. Her fear was real. Her voice, sharp.

Over time, the warnings softened.

Chitrarath-da no longer objected.

His father remained lost in his writing, distant and inward.

His mother devoted herself to teaching yoga and learning to the village children—sons and daughters of Nepali and Gorkha high-altitude porters.

The village itself was cut off from the world.

There were no roads.

To reach it, one had to cross the Gangotri Glacier. All contact with the outside world came through the air—by flight alone. And yet, within this isolation, the village thrived. Rare fruits grew here. Strange, nourishing foods sustained the people. They lived quietly. Strongly. Whole.

Every day, Gopal came to the black mountain to meditate.

What had once been a brief morning ritual became something else.

Hours passed. Then entire days.

Sometimes pilgrims passed by on their way to Gomukh, not far from here. They walked with purpose, eyes fixed ahead.

Gopal did not follow them.

His path was inward.

Toward the black mountain.

Toward its silence.

Toward the presence that watched without eyes.

Toward Mahākāla—

who waits beyond time,

and beyond fear.

Chapter Two: The First Omen

The wind changed first.

It was subtle—so subtle that only someone sitting in silence would notice. Gopal felt it brush against his skin, colder than before, sharper, as if the mountain had exhaled.

He opened his eyes.

The black mountain stood exactly as it always had—vast, still, unreadable. And yet, something was different. The silence had weight now. Not emptiness, but attention.

Gopal's breath slowed.

For the first time since he began meditating here, his thoughts did not wander. They did not resist. They stopped.

A single sound rose from the depths of the valley.

Not thunder.

Not wind.

Not a voice.

It was more like a pulse.

A low, rhythmic vibration that seemed to come from beneath the earth itself. The ground did not shake, but Gopal felt it in his chest, as though his heartbeat had momentarily aligned with something far larger.

He placed his palm on the stone beside him.

It was warm.

That should not have been possible.

Snow lingered on the higher ridges. The air was thin, unforgiving. Yet the rock beneath his hand carried a quiet heat—steady, alive.

Gopal withdrew his hand slowly.

Across the valley, a flock of birds lifted into the sky all at once, scattering without pattern, without direction. They vanished behind the white mountain, leaving the air abruptly empty.

Then it happened.

A thin line of light appeared on the black mountain's surface.

Not reflected light.

Not sunlight.

It was as if the mountain itself had opened one eye.

The line did not grow wider. It did not move. It simply was—a vertical mark, ancient and precise, like a forgotten symbol briefly remembering itself.

Gopal stood up.

His legs trembled, not from fear, but from recognition. Something within him knew this moment had already existed—somewhere beyond memory, beyond time.

Behind him, a voice spoke.

"You saw it too."

Gopal turned.

Chitrarath-da stood a few steps away, leaning on his walking staff. His face was pale. His eyes were not on Gopal—but on the mountain.

"The mark has not appeared in my lifetime," Chitrarath-da said softly. "Nor in my father's."

"What is it?" Gopal asked.

Chitrarath-da did not answer at once.

"When Mahākāla stirs," he finally said, "the world does not end.

It prepares."

The light on the mountain faded.

The warmth in the stone vanished.

The valley returned to its familiar stillness, as if nothing had happened at all.

But Gopal knew better.

Something had been acknowledged.

Something had been accepted.

That night, far beyond the valley, clocks across distant cities lost a second.

No one noticed.

Except Mahākāla. That a poetry came automatically to Gopal

as if a mantra uttered from higher planes.

Kalki Mahākāla

Before me stands

Mahākāla—

touching the depths of the ocean,

steadfast in the silence of mountains.

In his eyes

an unblinking radiance—

a fire that does not extinguish

even after countless falls.

The light in his hand

rests upon an island—

not unfamiliar,

yet never easily grasped.

There was a time

when the ground slipped beneath my feet,

when days grew shorter and narrower.

Those moments now survive

only as memories dissolved

into the voice of time.

For time

does not bring only erosion—

at times,

it slowly awakens

the strength within.

Those who assumed

every return has its end

never learned the language of time.

Time leaves its marks—

it does not erase.

The pen, then,

does more than write;

it sketches a moving design—

it does not shatter,

yet it opens a path.

Some powers

seek to imprison even silence,

forgetting—

that silence, too,

one day crosses beyond.

Time

never comes to a halt.

It merely

changes its name.

Those who once showed the way,

who taught battle within—

their Kurukshetra

was never on the map of the world.

It existed

deep within the mind—

in the space between

dharma and adharma.

That war

has not ended.

It returns

when time itself

seeks to recognize its own face.

What truly belongs

remains standing.

And what does not—

in the current of time,

falls away

on its own.

Chapter Three: The Mantra He Never Learned

The dream came before sleep after he wrote the poetry.

Gopal lay awake in the dim light of the oil lamp, listening to the slow breathing of the house. Outside, the wind had stilled. Even the mountain seemed to be waiting.

Then the words arose.

Not as sound.

Not as thought.

They surfaced from somewhere below language, forming themselves inside his breath.

His chest tightened.

A rhythm began—steady, ancient, unmistakable. Each inhalation carried a syllable he did not recognize, yet somehow knew. His tongue moved without instruction. His lips shaped sounds no one had ever taught him.

The mantra spoke itself.

Gopal sat up abruptly.

The lamp flickered. The flame bent sideways, as if responding to something unseen. Sweat ran down his spine, though the air was cold.

He pressed his palms together.

The mantra continued.

It did not ask permission.

He tried to stop it.

The moment he resisted, pain bloomed behind his eyes. His heartbeat quickened, then slowed, then aligned again with that same deep rhythm he had felt at the mountain.

A memory—not his—flashed through him.

Ash.

A horizon burning red.

A blade buried in stone.

Gopal gasped.

The mantra broke.

Silence crashed into the room, heavier than sound.

Outside, a dog howled once—and then went quiet.

Gopal's hands were trembling.

He had studied chants. He knew the structure of sacred sound. This was different. This mantra did not descend from lineage. It did not belong to any school, any scripture he had learned.

It had recognized him.

At dawn, he went to find Chitrarath-da.

The old man was already awake, seated beside the fire, eyes half-closed.

"You heard it," Chitrarath-da said, before Gopal could speak.

"I don't know it," Gopal replied. "I was never taught."

Chitrarath-da opened his eyes.

"That is how you know it is real."

He reached into a cloth bundle and pulled out a thin copper plate, darkened with age. Upon it was etched a symbol—simple, severe.

A vertical line.

The same mark Gopal had seen on the mountain.

"This is not a mantra meant to be remembered," Chitrarath-da said. "It is meant to awaken when the time arrives."

"Whose mantra is it?" Gopal asked.

Chitrarath-da's gaze hardened.

"Not yours," he said. "Not yet."

He placed the copper plate back into the fire. The metal did not melt.

Smoke rose straight upward, defying the wind.

"When Mahākāla begins to speak," Chitrarath-da continued, "he does not speak to the world. He speaks to one who must learn to listen."

Gopal felt the echo of the mantra stir again—soft now, restrained.

Waiting.

That evening, in a city far from the mountains, a child recited a chant no one had taught him.

And somewhere beyond time, Mahākāla turned his face.

Chapter Four: The One Who Should Not Be Named

Names were never spoken here.

Not aloud.

Not fully.

In Jñānagañja, certain words were carried like fire—useful only when held with care. Some names, the elders said, bent the air when uttered. Others awakened what should remain asleep.

This was one of them.

That evening, the sky darkened too early. Clouds gathered without wind, pressing low against the mountains. The black peak vanished behind a curtain of shadow.

Gopal sat with Chitrarath-da and two other elders by the low fire. No one spoke for a long time. The silence felt deliberate.

Finally, one of the elders broke it.

“The mark has appeared,” he said. “And the boy hears the sound.”

Chitrarath-da nodded once.

“Then the sealed name is stirring.”

The fire crackled sharply, as if in warning.

Gopal felt the mantra shift inside him—tighten, coil, retreat.

“Who?” he asked.

No one answered.

Chitrarath-da looked at him then—not with fear, but with gravity.

“There are beings,” he said, “who exist between ending and beginning. They are not born. They return.”

He drew a circle in the ash with his staff, then broke it with a line through the center.

“When the age rots from within,” he continued, “such a being does not arrive as savior. He arrives as correction.”

Gopal’s breath caught.

“You speak of—”

Chitrarath-da raised his hand.

“Do not name him.”

The mountain answered.

A low sound rolled through the valley—not loud, but deep enough to be felt in the bones. The elders bowed their heads instinctively.

“This is why names were sealed,” one of them whispered. “Because to name is to summon.”

Gopal stared toward the black mountain.

In its shadow, he felt something ancient shift its attention—slow, immense, patient.

That night, Chitrarath-da took Gopal to a chamber carved into stone beneath the village. The air smelled of copper and ash.

On the wall were markings—old, worn, deliberate.

No stories.

No praise.

Only warnings.

Chitrarath-da pointed to a carving of a figure without a face, holding neither weapon nor scripture.

“He appears when the world forgets restraint,” he said. “When dharma becomes performance. When power pretends to be virtue.”

“Is he divine?” Gopal asked.

Chitrarath-da hesitated.

“He is necessary.”

Gopal felt the mantra stir again—stronger now, pressing against his breath.

“And if he is awakened?” Gopal asked.

Chitrarath-da met his gaze.

“Then no one remains unchanged,” he said. “Not even the one who carries his call.”

Above them, the black mountain stood unseen.

Listening.

Chapter Five: The First Trial Is Silence

The trial did not begin with fire.

It began with nothing.

At dawn, Chitrarath-da led Gopal away from the village, past the last stone shrine and into a narrow ravine where sound seemed to thin and fade. The black mountain loomed above, unseen but unmistakably present.

“This is not a place of teaching,” Chitrarath-da said. “It is a place of withholding.”

He pointed to a flat slab of stone.

“Sit.”

Gopal obeyed.

“No mantra,” Chitrarath-da continued. “No breath-control. No invocation. You will not call. You will not answer.”

“For how long?” Gopal asked.

Chitrarath-da did not reply.

The elders withdrew.

Silence closed in.

At first, it was ordinary—the absence of speech, the quiet of windless air. Gopal listened to his own breath, to the distant echo of water somewhere far below.

Then silence deepened.

Time loosened its grip.

Thoughts rose and dissolved without effort. Sensations blurred. His body felt both heavy and distant, as if it were slowly forgetting itself.

That was when the mantra returned.

It pressed against him, urgent now, demanding release. The syllables gathered at his lips, ready to spill into sound.

Gopal resisted.

Pain followed.

Not sharp—insistent. A pressure behind the sternum, a tightening around the skull. His muscles twitched, begging for movement, for expression.

The mountain remained silent.

Hours—or something like them—passed.

Gopal felt anger rise. Then fear. Then longing. Each emotion came with its own argument, its own justification to speak, to chant, to act.

He did none of it.

When exhaustion set in, something shifted.

The mantra loosened its grip.

In its place came something else—not sound, not thought, but space. A vast inner stillness, untouched by effort or will.

Within that stillness, Gopal sensed a presence.

It did not instruct.

It did not comfort.

It did not demand.

It simply was.

As dusk approached, Chitrarath-da returned.

He studied Gopal's face carefully.

"You did not answer," he said.

Gopal shook his head.

"You did not speak," Chitrarath-da continued.

Gopal remained silent.

Chitrarath-da nodded once.

"Then the mountain has heard you."

That night, the black mountain did not call.

And for the first time since the omen appeared, Mahākāla waited.

Chapter Six : The Refusal to become Kalki

The Black Mountain does not speak to Gopal.

Yet he knows—it listens.

Leaning against its stone body, he has burned with anger many times, and fallen into silence just as often.

The mountain does not ask questions.

It does not judge.

Here, Gopal feels least alone.

The White Mountain stands far away.

Not in distance of land, but of the mind.

Still, Gopal has discovered a shortcut—

a narrow path that leads quickly to the Shivling Mountain.

He shows this path to no one.

It belongs to him, as he belongs to no rule.

He is nineteen.

At this age, he feels that whatever he says, no one truly hears.

In this mountain settlement, education is fragile and the economy even more so.

No one here is prepared to step into the larger world.

And Gopal—

he has spent years immersed in spiritual discipline.

At times, he wonders if this discipline has made him invisible.

In his mother Suranjana's eyes, he is still a child—a responsibility.

But in his own eyes, he has already crossed that threshold.

Respect feels like a word slowly disappearing from his life.

The older he grows, the clearer it becomes—he is different.

The work of this village is physical, repetitive; its thinking confined.

Here, no one truly understands his inner awakening.

His father remains absorbed in his own pursuits.

His mother watches over him carefully, afraid to let him go.

She knows what Gopal has attained through his austerities in the depths of the Black Mountain—

the Eight Siddhis, the force of mantra—

power that could become dangerous in the wrong hands.

If he leaves this place, his path may collide with the influence of Kali.

His mother senses it.

She sees something forming inside her son.

The presence of Kalki seems to be awakening—slowly, inevitably.

Most of the time, Gopal is calm.

When he meditates, a deep stillness settles within him.

And yet, without warning, he can feel utterly ordinary—almost insignificant.

His father's books, the internet—these open windows beyond the mountains.

Kolkata appears there not as a city, but as a current—

argument, ambition, hunger, ideology, noise.

In this age, war is no longer fought only with weapons.

In this age, spirituality is no longer contained in scriptures alone.

Science has pushed the outer world forward at a pace once unimaginable.

Gopal understands this.

That is why many practices taught by ascetics feel outdated to him—

echoes of superstition rather than truth.

Poverty is his constant companion.

The income from his father's books arrives slowly, sometimes after years.

Loneliness, financial strain, and the inability to share his inner struggles—

together they ignite a quiet fire within him.

The people here speak Nepali.

Gopal speaks the language fluently.

Yet emotion does not translate so easily.

Despite everything, he feels free.

And within that freedom, he searches for one thing—

a friend who might understand.

Someone with whom he can share his doubts, his conflicts, his fears.

Yet when the thought comes—

that he may be meant for something larger—

Gopal resists it.

He has seen what happens to men who believe they are chosen.

In Kolkata, they become leaders or lunatics.

In the Himalayas, they become gods too early—or corpses.

Sambhala, the hidden kingdom spoken of in fragments, is not a place of arrival.

It is a place of restraint.

Those who seek it openly are never permitted to enter.

Gopal tells himself he does not want power.

He does not want prophecy.

He does not want to be another name consumed by belief.

If Kalki is awakening, let it awaken elsewhere.

Let it pass through time without touching him.

He presses his forehead against the Black Mountain and breathes.

“I am not ready,” he thinks—not as prayer, but as refusal.

Then—

On the path of the Black Mountain, he notices someone standing.

A stranger.

Silent.

Her face half-veiled in light and shadow.

The wind shifts direction.

The mountain seems to pause, as if holding its breath.

Gopal cannot explain why, but he knows—

this meeting is not accidental.

And still, he takes a step back.

This girl—

the first answer to the call he has tried to deny.

But even before her name is spoken,

Gopal understands something with unsettling clarity:

The call of Kalki does not ask for permission.

It only waits—for the refusal to be exhausted.

Chapter Seven: Meeting Sutapa

That day, when Gopal saw Sutapa, he was truly astonished.

On the far side of the Black Mountain—where the Shivling-shaped White Mountain rose in silent contrast—a lone girl was sitting in deep meditation. There were no signs of human presence, no traces of animals, no paths worn by feet. It was far from their small village of Sambala, far beyond even the scattered settlements near the Black Mountain. Such solitude was almost unimaginable.

From a distance, Gopal watched her—still as stone, absorbed, unmoving. A little away from her lay a small tent, and beside it a black jacket. Against the white mountain, her meditating figure appeared strangely beautiful, as if the landscape itself had paused to observe her.

At first, Gopal hesitated. Then, crossing the valley, he began to walk toward her.

Growing up among Gorkha Nepalese, Gopal had never lacked courage. And whenever something unfamiliar appeared before him, an invisible pull drew him toward it. I should speak to her, he thought.

His mind wandered briefly—to stories he had heard from Chitrada about his father Subimal Ray's solitary journeys, undertaken in silence, without informing anyone, on nights filled with strange portents. There were also whispers of the Chitra Samhita, from where—so it was said—some had foretold Gopal's birth and the future of the world.

Gopal never believed anything blindly. He needed certainty—depth, logic, experience. His father admired this habit, though his mother often argued with him over it. Many teachers, she said, would come into his life. One of them, perhaps, had already arrived.

The girl ended her meditation, opened her eyes, and stared steadily at the White Mountain.

Gathering his courage, Gopal approached the rock on which she had been sitting and asked, "Did you come from Gomukh?"

Beyond Gomukh lay a world Gopal knew almost nothing about. Since birth, he had never crossed the Gangotri glacier.

The girl smiled. "Kolkata," she said. Then added with another smile, "Though my home is actually in Bardhaman."

She looked radiant—youthful, alive.

"What is Kolkata like?" Gopal asked.

She replied, "It's the opposite of this place. Here, no one speaks—everything is silent. There, people talk all the time. They argue, debate, discuss, protest, quarrel, march in processions. Kolkata is never quiet."

"But we are speaking now," Gopal said calmly. "Maybe the people you met here didn't know your language."

"Maybe," she laughed. "But how did you learn Bengali?"

"My mother is Bengali—Suranjana Ganguly. My father is Subimal Ray. And I am Gopal Ray."

Her expression changed.

"Subimal Ray—the great journalist? The one who could sense events before they happened? He once headed the world's largest news network. A brilliant writer… though he hasn't written for years. I heard he left everything behind and disappeared somewhere in the Himalayas."

"Yes," Gopal said softly. "Father doesn't want anyone to know where he lives."

"No, no—this can't be that I become this far and don't meet him!" she said. "When I was studying journalism at Jadavpur University, he came to give a lecture on writing. He knows me well."

"Then come to our village," Gopal said. "It's far from here. If you don't want to come back . You can stay with us."

"But our team has already arrived," she hesitated. "Two people from your village are part of our high-altitude porter. Should we go today? No one knows how late Bidyut Da will return."

"He is our team leader though he is an mechanical engineer and he is bit eccentric suddenly he can say 'Sutapa, why stay at Base Camp? Let's come with us in Camp One'. But I'll regret coming all this way and not meeting Subimal Ray."

"Your name is Sutapa?" Gopal asked.

"Yes In December,I did a rock climbing course" she said. "Then Rajib, one of our mountaineers, fell ill. Vidyut da called me and said, 'Sutapa, you must go.' My boss agreed immediately when I said I will send articles every day about my journey"

"Our travel magazine is publishing a special issue," she continued. "I've been sending daily dispatches. Today's article is complete—but there's no bandwidth here."

"This mountain blocks all bandwidth," Gopal said. "But Father has a satellite phone. He sends his manuscripts to publishers through it. You can use that."

Talking endlessly, they walked toward the village. After nearly an hour, they reached Gopal's home.

Subimal Ray was sitting at his writing desk, deeply engrossed. Suranjana was busy teaching children—boys and girls from nearby villages. Chitrarath da-da was preparing food.

Stepping inside, Sutapa felt as though she had entered an intensely Bengali world—deep in a foreign land. Everyone spoke flawless Bengali; the cooking was extraordinary. Chitrarath da, though Odia by origin, was a master cook.

The house was small, calm, almost ascetic. Nothing could be easily brought here—supplies had to be carried across Gangotri or flown in by helicopter. Yet beside the house was a helipad, with a helicopter resting on it—no surprise, given that Subimal Ray was among the most influential and wealthy figures in the region.

Solar panels lined the tin roof, powering the entire house. It contained modern electronic equipment—and even robots that handled household work.

Here lived one of the world's most celebrated writers of mythology and science fiction—hidden in a village like Sambala.

There was a vast library. Sutapa was shown Gopal's study, and Suranjana's alternative education centre.

Using the satellite phone, Sutapa sent her article to her publisher. She stayed briefly, then returned to her tent, promising to come back the next day. Subimal asked Gopal to accompany her.

Vidyut-da's accident forced Sutapa to return early from Base Camp. By then, she had fallen in love with Gopal. And Gopal, too, had fallen in love with her.

Subimal and Suranjana felt a familiar unease—the very reason they had chosen to live far from human settlements resurfaced. They did not want Gopal to leave. Only Suranjana voiced her fears.

Yet Gopal remained firm. He wanted to see the moving world beyond the village.

Finally, as a resolution, Chitra rath da stepped forward. He decided to go with Subimal himself.

Chapter Eight: Kolkata - The City Where Silence Is Impossible

The city never slept.

Even before sunrise, its veins were alive—screens flickering, engines humming, voices overlapping without listening. Sound layered upon sound until silence became unimaginable.

Gopal arrived with nothing but a small cloth bag and the weight of the mountain stillness inside him.

The air felt thick. Not with dust—but with urgency.

People moved quickly, eyes fixed ahead or downward, fingers in constant motion. Words were exchanged in fragments. Laughter rose and vanished without warmth.

This, Chitrarath-da had said, would be the real test.

Here, no one asked you to speak.

They demanded it.

Gopal found a place to sit near a crowded crossing. A screen above him pulsed with headlines—conflict, outrage, spectacle. Images shifted too fast to remember.

A voice beside him laughed.

“Quiet, huh?” the man said. “You new here?”

Gopal nodded.

The man kept talking anyway.

Opinions poured out—about politics, faith, money, enemies no one had seen but everyone blamed. Gopal listened without reply.

The man grew uncomfortable.

“You don’t have much to say,” he muttered, moving away.

By noon, the pressure built.

The mantra stirred again—not as revelation, but as reaction. Each shout, each lie repeated loudly, pulled at it, urging release. A single word from Gopal, spoken at the right moment, could have gathered attention. Could have commanded.

He remained silent.

In the afternoon, a crowd gathered.

An argument had escalated. Accusations flew. Someone fell. Phones rose in unison, recording rather than helping.

Gopal stepped forward.

He did not chant.

He did not shout.

He placed himself between two men, eyes steady, breath calm.

Something shifted.

The shouting faltered—not because it was stopped, but because it was seen. One man stepped back. Another lowered his voice.

The crowd dispersed, disappointed.

That night, alone in a small room, Gopal felt the cost of the day. His body ached. His mind buzzed. Silence here was not empty—it was resisted.

He sat on the floor and did nothing.

No mantra came.

No vision.

Only fatigue—and beneath it, resolve.

Far above the city, a satellite lost its signal for three seconds.

No system failed.

No alert sounded.

But somewhere beyond time, Mahākāla marked the moment.

Silence had entered the city.

And the city had not noticed.

Chapter Nine : The Weapon That Refuses a Hand

The weapon was not hidden.

That was the first mistake people made when they spoke of it.

It did not sleep in stone.

It was not guarded by fire.

No prophecy pointed to a chosen bearer.

It waited.

Gopal found it by accident—or what the world calls accident.

At the edge of the city stood an abandoned structure, once a place of assembly. Its walls were layered with posters—leaders promising order, voices demanding justice, slogans that had lost their meaning through repetition.

Inside, the air was still.

Too still.

At the center of the hall stood a low platform. Upon it rested a long, narrow object wrapped in dark cloth. No glow. No sound. No warning.

Gopal did not reach for it.

He circled the platform slowly, aware of a pressure building in his chest—not urgency, but resistance. The mantra did not stir. The silence inside him tightened.

Finally, he stopped.

The cloth slipped on its own.

Beneath it lay a blade.

Simple. Unadorned. Neither ancient nor modern. Its surface reflected nothing clearly, as if refusing interpretation.

Gopal extended his hand.

The moment his fingers came close, the air thickened. His arm felt heavy—immovable. Not pain. Not fear.

Rejection.

He withdrew his hand.

The pressure eased.

Footsteps echoed behind. Suddenly he find Sutapa.

"You felt it," her voice said.

Sutapa stood near the doorway. Her eyes were sharp, measuring. She carried herself like someone accustomed to command.

"It doesn't accept intention," she continued. "Only alignment."

"Whose weapon is it?" Gopal asked.

She smiled faintly.

"Everyone wants it to be theirs."

She stepped forward and reached for the blade.

The platform shuddered.

The blade did not move.

Her smile vanished.

"This weapon does not respond to desire," she said quietly. "Nor ambition. Nor righteousness performed for an audience."

She looked at Gopal.

"It responds to restraint."

Gopal said nothing.

"That is why it will not come to you yet," she added. "And why it frightens those who seek it."

"Why show it to me?" Gopal asked.

"Because Mahākāla has begun to withdraw permission," she replied. "Soon, even the unworthy will no longer be able to see it."

She turned to leave.

"At the moment it accepts a hand," she said over her shoulder, "the world will lose its excuses."

When the hall fell silent again, the blade remained.

Unclaimed.

Unmoved.

Unimpressed.

Far away, in a place where decisions were traded like currency, a powerful man woke suddenly, gripping his hand in pain—though no wound was visible.

The weapon had refused him too.

And Mahākāla continued to wait.

.

Chapter Ten: Sutapa Knows the Seals

Her name was not given.

Names, Sutapa said, create expectations. And expectations distort listening.

Gopal met her again at dusk he and Chitra rath da was staying at her flat, far from the abandoned hall. The city had begun to glow—lights rising like a second sky, louder than the stars they replaced.

"You followed," she said, without turning.

"I listened," Gopal replied.

That earned him a brief glance.

They walked in silence until the noise thinned and the buildings gave way to an old quarter of narrow lanes and closed doors. At the end of the last alley stood a structure that did not belong to any time.

Stone. Plain. Unmarked.

She pressed her palm against the wall.

Nothing happened.

Then she placed her other hand over her heart and exhaled slowly. Her breath was steady, deliberate. The wall responded—not by opening, but by remembering.

A seam appeared.

Inside, the air was cool and still, like the mountain.

“This place is sealed,” she said. “Not locked. Seals are agreements, not barriers.”

Inside, the room was circular. On the walls were symbols etched deep into the stone—lines, curves, breaks, repetitions. Some Gopal recognized. Others felt familiar without explanation.

“You saw the blade,” she said. “It refused you.”

“Yes.”

“Good,” she replied. “If it had not, we would be in trouble.”

She traced one symbol with her finger—a broken circle intersected by a vertical line.

“Seals exist to prevent acceleration,” she said. “Not destruction. The world does not end because of weapons. It ends because of haste.”

“Who placed them?” Gopal asked.

She paused.

“Those who survived the last correction.”

She faced him fully now.

“You carry the sound,” she said. “Not because you are chosen—but because you are unclaimed.”

Gopal felt the mantra stir, restrained but awake.

“What do you want from me?” he asked.

“To keep refusing,” she said. “As long as possible.”

She reached into a pouch and removed a thin metal disc, etched with the same vertical mark.

“This is a seal-key,” she said. “It does not open doors. It closes them—when needed.”

She placed it in his palm.

It was neither warm nor cold.

“Why me?” Gopal asked again.

She met his gaze.

“Because Mahākāla does not trust those who hurry,” she said. “And the seals are failing.”

A distant tremor passed through the ground—not violent, but deliberate.

Somewhere in the city, a monument cracked without falling.

“The first seal will break soon,” she said. “When it does, noise will claim authority.”

She stepped back into the shadow of the wall.

“When the weapon finally accepts a hand,” she added, “it will not be because someone reached for it.”

“It will be because someone stopped.”

The seam in the stone closed.

Gopal stood alone in the narrow lane, the seal-key heavy in his palm.

Above the city, the sky flickered once.

And far beyond sight, Mahākāla began to count as Kali prepared to give his

Blow.

Chapter Eleven : The Memory Before Birth

Kali did not descend into Kolkata.

He unfolded within it. As Gopal thought the seal key is his gift of the Mahakal Tapasya in this life. He was surprised to find things in other way.

The city was already prepared—its veins humming with restless light, its nights breathing unresolved arguments, its alleys coiled with ambition, hunger, devotion, rage. Kolkata had always been a living yantra, its geometry imperfect, its rhythm broken—ideal for Kali.

At midnight, when tram wires slept and the Hooghly held its breath, Kali traced a circle not on land, but on intention.

From that intention arose the Chakravyūha.

Not the ancient wheel of war—but its final mutation.

A Charuvyūha:

a seductive spiral of narratives, screens, slogans, half-truths, algorithms, nostalgia, outrage, and faith weaponized into performance.

There were no soldiers.

Only opinions.

No conch shells.

Only notifications.

At its core shimmered a seal—neither mantra nor machine—whose seal key is with Gopal (Kalki) now.

a sigil forged from forgotten vows.

Kali pressed the seal into the city.

And the city opened.

The Entry of Gopal with Sutapa with the seal with Chitrarath Da as his mentor.

He was taken aback and he asked Chitrarath .

“Think hard it must be in your memory by now with Mahakalas blessings. The mantra silently invokes all the important merit and awareness from your past lives”

Gopal did not walk into the Charuvyūha.

He remembered his way in.

The memory did not belong to this life.

It came from before breath.

From a night in the Himalayas, long before he was born—

when Suranjana slept beside Subimal,

and the fire dimmed,

and words spoken were not meant for waking ears.

Suranjana had said softly, half-dreaming:

"If you are truly Arjuna reborn,

then tell me this—

how does one enter and leave the Chakravyūha?"

There had been a pause.

A deep one.

The kind that bends time.

And then Subimal spoke again—but the voice was older.

"I never told Uttara how to come out.

That secret was sealed with Abhimanyu's breath.

But I will tell you—

because the one who is coming

will fight a battle far worse than Kurukshetra."

Suranjana, still asleep, turned slightly.

The Forgotten Teaching

“Listen carefully, Draupadī.

Your son will remember this when the time comes.”

“A Chakravyūha is not broken by force.

It collapses when identity refuses to perform its role.”

“Entry requires desire—

the desire to prove, to fight, to correct, to save.”

“Exit requires disobedience—

the refusal to complete the script.”

“Inside the wheel, everything will provoke you:

injustice, suffering, blasphemy, false compassion.”

“If you respond as a warrior,

the wheel tightens.”

“If you respond as a savior,

the wheel consumes.”

“The only way out—

is to remember that the wheel feeds on reaction.”

“Step inward when asked to rush forward.

Become silent when summoned to shout.

Refuse the center when offered the throne."

"And above all—

never forget:

the Chakravyūha collapses

when the one inside remembers

why he did not come to win."

The fire had gone out.

The Himalayas listened.

And the womb remembered.

Kalki Awakens as Gopal now.

Now, in Kolkata, Gopal stood within the Charuvyūha.

Screens flashed prophecies.

Crowds chanted half-mantras.

Saints argued like politicians.

Politicians wore saffron like armor.

Every path promised justice—

each leading deeper into the spiral.

Kali smiled.

"This is worse than war," he whispered.

"No arrows. No blood. Only belief."

Gopal closed his eyes.

He did not search for an exit.

He remembered why he had entered.

Not to defeat Kali.

Not to purify the age.

Not to restore a past that no longer existed.

But to end the wheel itself.

He pressed the seal—not outward, but inward and invoked the silent mantra which took him beyond time beyond return.

And the Charuvyūha faltered as it is made in time and it cannot press himself in front a awareness and a merit within a body which is beyond time and beyond return.

Because it had never learned

how to imprison someone

who did not seek victory as he is timeless by Mahakalas mantra blessings.

Gopal walked out the way he had entered—

through timeless memory,

through timeless refusal,

through compassion that did not perform.

Behind him, the city continued.

Trams rang.

Debates resumed.

Kali dissolved—not defeated, but postponed.

Because this was not the final battle.

Only the last warning.

Epilogue

That night, Suranjana woke suddenly.

She did not know why.

But she whispered into the dark:

“You remembered.”

Somewhere in Kolkata, Gopal smiled.

The age of destruction had not ended.

But the knowledge to survive it

had returned.

And that was enough—

for now.

Appendix

Kalki Mahakal is published by Sri Joydip Ashram Publications which conduct courses on some of the spiritual experience of Kalki Mahakal. Here is the Course path for experiencing that.

Sri Joydip Ashram Course Path – A Structured Approach to Yogic Learning and Healing

The Sri Joydip Ashram Learning Path: A Journey of Self-Realization, Healing, and Teaching

At **Sri Joydip Ashram**, yoga is not merely a practice—it is a **sacred journey of transformation**, guiding individuals toward **self-healing, expanded consciousness, and professional mastery**. Our structured course path offers a **progressive immersion** into the wisdom of **Surya Yoga and Gyan Yoga**, empowering students to evolve from seekers to **certified teachers of higher consciousness**.

1. Foundational Course: The Lifewise Program

◈ *Awakening Conscious Living Through Yoga*

The **Lifewise Program** is the **gateway to self-discovery** at Sri Joydip Ashram, designed for adult learners seeking to integrate yoga into their daily lives. Rooted in the **seven yoga habits**, this program nurtures **mental clarity, emotional resilience, and inner harmony**.

📌 **Structure:**

- **Duration:** 12 classes (24 hours) over one month
- **Investment:**
  - □12,000 (pay-per-class)
  - □10,000 (full advance payment, metropolitan cities)

📌 **Key Benefits:**

✓ Mastering **mindfulness and breathwork** to cultivate emotional balance

✓ Strengthening **mental resilience** against stress and anxiety

✓ Enhancing **energy alignment** for sustained well-being

Scientific research affirms that **regular yoga practice** fosters **neurological balance, stress reduction, and heightened cognitive function** (Khalsa et al., 2015; Field, 2011). Many students report profound shifts—**greater clarity, emotional stability, and an expanded sense of presence**.

2. Young Minds Program: Yoga for Youth Empowerment

◈ *Shaping Future Leaders with Clarity and Strength*

Designed for **students and young adults**, the **Young Minds Program** is a powerful tool for **intellectual and emotional empowerment**. It provides young learners with the **inner discipline** to navigate modern challenges while enhancing their **cognitive and emotional intelligence**.

Structure:

- **15 Classes** tailored for youth development

Core Transformations:

✓ **Increased concentration** and academic performance

✓ **Greater self-awareness** and emotional intelligence

✓ **Inner resilience** to face academic and social pressures

Research by **Harvard Medical School (2016)** highlights that yoga **boosts memory, attention, and cognitive function**, making it a **powerful accelerator of youth potential**.

3. Customizable Healing & Deep Practice Courses

◈ *Personalized Pathways for Self-Healing & Growth*

Upon completing foundational training, students can customize their practice, choosing specific **healing-oriented courses** based on their unique needs.

📍 **Options:**

✓ **12-class deep practice blocks** for progressive Surya Yoga mastery

✓ **Healing-focused courses** tailored for mental and physical well-being

A **Stanford University (2019) study** on sunlight exposure underscores the **scientific foundation** of **Surya Yoga's solar-based techniques**, showing their profound effects on **mood regulation, circadian rhythm balance, and energy restoration**.

---

4. Advanced Training: The Teacher's Path to Mastery

◈ *Becoming a Torchbearer of Yoga Wisdom*

For those drawn to **share the light of yoga**, Sri Joydip Ashram offers **two levels of teacher certification**, designed to cultivate **profound wisdom, teaching expertise, and mastery of Surya Yoga**.

🔎 **Lifewise Teachers Training Program (200 Hours)**

✔ **Duration:** 21 days

✔ **Investment:** □50,000

✔ **Core Training:**

- Deep immersion in **yoga philosophy & mindfulness practices**
- Mastery of **asana sequencing, breathwork, and teaching techniques**
- Development of **holistic teaching methodology**

❇ *Outcome:* Graduates emerge as **competent instructors**, capable of guiding students with an **integrated approach to yoga and self-transformation**.

🔎 **2. Advanced Teachers Training Program (500 Hours)**

✔ **Duration:** 48 days

✔ **Investment:** □80,000

✔ **Advanced Training:**

- Profound Surya Yoga **energy mastery**
- Therapeutic applications for **mental and emotional healing**
- Teaching expertise aligned with **global certification standards**

❀ *Outcome:* This program prepares **world-class yoga educators** who can teach in **wellness centers, corporate programs, international retreats, and therapeutic settings**.

A Journey Beyond Teaching—A Path to Higher Consciousness

At **Sri Joydip Ashram**, yoga is not a mere discipline but a **way of being**—a journey into the depths of **self-awareness, energy alignment, and inner mastery**. Every course is meticulously structured to **awaken the seeker, empower the practitioner, and refine the teacher**, ensuring that each student experiences:

✨ **Physical rejuvenation through Surya Yoga's solar energy alignment**
✨ **Mental clarity and emotional balance through Gyan Yoga's wisdom practices**
✨ **Spiritual awakening through conscious living and self-realization**

By making **profound yoga education accessible and transformative**, Sri Joydip Ashram **empowers individuals** to lead **enlightened, purposeful, and balanced lives**—as both **practitioners of self-healing** and **teachers of higher consciousness**.

Are you ready to embark on this **sacred journey of transformation?**

Kalki Mahakal
Sri Joydip

Authors Bio

Sri Joydip is a consciousness educator, author, filmmaker, and cultural practitioner working at the intersection of ethics, mental health, and lived spirituality.

With over two decades of experience, he is the founder of Sri Joydip Ashram Gyan Yoga Training & Research Centre and the creator of the Seven Yoga Habits and Lifewise frameworks—widely used for addressing anxiety, OCD, addiction, burnout, and moral fatigue through structured inner discipline rather than motivational rhetoric.

He is the author of multiple acclaimed books, including Seven Yoga habits That Can Transform Your Life, Arunachala Diaries: Living a Different Reality, Science of Yoga, Neem Baba, Lifewise: Yoga Recipe for Living Wisely, Living Wisely with Meditation,and Buddha: Art of Mindfulness.

His work is used as course material in institutional settings and has been internationally recognized for its depth and practicality.

A long-time participant in India's cultural ecosystem, his films have been screened at major festivals, including the Kolkata International Film Festival.

Sri Joydip's work emphasizes ethical wellness, cultural responsibility, and the recovery of wisdom in an age of distraction.

www.ingramcontent.com/pod-product-compliance
Lightning Source LLC
Chambersburg PA
CBHW062147160726
48282CB00027B/948
* 9 7 8 8 1 9 7 2 6 1 9 4 7 *